# A LOVE HAPPENED OVER COFFEE!

## A ROMANTIC POCKETSTORY!

## SURYAKANTH

This book is dedicated to all the love couples out there!

# Contents

# Acknowledgements

It's been an year, haven't released any books in that period. I got catched up with some personal works, pursuing my master degree, enhancing my skillset required for the corporate world. Fortunately i'm doing well enough and now i think i have to return to the world of my writings, so I'm here back to creating fictional realities!

There's a lot of stories to be published which has been delayed a lot. I'll try to publish all of them one by one perfectly to you, my readers.

Thanks to my family, friends, teachers & professors, well-wishers, readers and followers for always supporting and staying with me no matter what happens. Thanks a lot!

# Prologue

Our elders have a saying that a good thing happens when somebody faces a bad situation. And this is very much true, we all have seen and felt this at some point in our life. The situations may differ but the emotion is the same for everyone. In this story, Shantanu goes through a tragic situation but how his life turned into a pure bliss by meeting Elyse is our story!

Shantanu Rajsekhar, recently got his first job. So he decided to keep this good news as a surprise to his girlfriend Poorna Chandrakant. Shantanu decided to break this good news to Poorna at a cafe shop at Bandra. Elyse Charles, was working at a private company at Bandra, how both Shantanu and Elyse are connected, how they met, how they move further after meeting, and how a love happened over coffee is our story!

# CHAPTER ONE

# SURPRISE TURNS TO TRAGEDY

In the busy streets of Bandra, in a coffee shop there was Shantanu discussing something with a waiter of that cafe about his plan.

"Brother, I need you to bring this ring sharply at 9.05 PM here and serve us your famous cone coffee with writings on it as 'will you be my better half, sweetheart?' and that too with some celebratory mood."

"Don't worry sir, we got you! Everything will go as planned! Just give us a hint or a signal when mam arrives!"

"Sure, thanks for the help brother!"

"It's our pleasure to help you, sir!"

Yes, what you guessed is right. Shantanu is going to propose to the love of his life Poorna, tonight with a surprise news. Shantanu has got into a good job with a decent salary package. And this is the first ever job in his life and he wanted to share this first with Poorna.

Shantanu texted Poorna about where she was, and in reply Poorna texted that she'll call him back in 2 minutes. In that meantime, Shantanu called his friend Mohit to inform about a plan.

"Mohit, this is Shantanu here!"

"Yes bro, wassup?"

"I'm arranging a party tomorrow, so you're the first person I'm inviting to this."

"Good to hear about a party being arranged after a long time in our friends' gang. What's the matter for the party tomorrow?"

"I'll let you know the reason tonight bro, it may be double good news! Let's hope for the best to happen, Mohit."

"Hmm... then something big is gonna happen tonight with you, fingers crossed bro. Wishing you all the very best with what you are up to."

"Thanks Mohit, i'll call you later tonight!"

During that on-going call, Poorna was also trying to call Shantanu. So he hung up the call with Mohit and called back Poorna.

"Hey Poorna, I was talking with Mohit about some arrangements tomorrow. So that's why I couldn't attend your call."

"It's fine, Shantanu. I just called to say something important."

"Keep it aside for now Poorna, by the way where are you now? I've been waiting for you in the cafe for a while."

"That is what I wanted to talk about, Shantanu. I'm not coming to the cafe now."

"Not coming means you're busy with something, Poorna?"

"Actually I'm not, but I think I shouldn't be there now, Shantanu."

"Please come to the point Poorna, what is more important to you than our date?"

"It's not working between us, Shantanu. It's been months I've been trying to rectify the missing part of our relationship and I think now I've figured it out."

"Hold on a sec, what are you trying to convey now, Poorna?"

"Let's break up, Shantanu. You're still living in the cool bachelor mode and you're not thinking about the next step in life."

"For this reason you're breaking our relationship, Poorna? Are you for real now?"

"You know my friend's boyfriend gifted her a new Iphone. My sister's fiance bought a new diamond necklace for her. What have you done for me?"

"Poorna, this doesn't match with the reason you gave earlier. This seems like you're more focused on spending money on a girlfriend."

"Yes, I want someone who could spend money for me, for my happiness. And you're not the person I expect to be, Shantanu."

"So money is more important than my love, Poorna? Can you justify this?"

"For how long will you spend your love on me? Will only love make me happy, Shantanu?"

"This is what every person expects from their lover, and I did my best to keep you happy and safe."

"Shantanu, there is no time for me to explain this philosophy to you now. Let's finish here itself. Do you have anything left to say?"

"You've already made up your mind Poorna, I got nothing more left. Hope you get a boyfriend as you expected."

"Fine, Bye Shantanu."

Poorna ends the call, Shantanu was devastated by hearing the unjustifiable words of Poorna. He never thought a situation like this would occur in his life. Shantanu wanted to give good news to his love, but in return he got a heartbroke statement. Shantanu stood up and left the cafe immediately. He walked as fast as possible and headed towards the Bandstand Sea Face view.

# CHAPTER TWO

# THANKS, CHURCH FATHER!

Elyse was returning from home from work, this was her first day. So she decided to visit the church and get blessing from the church father whom she last met almost 8 years ago. Elyse left Mumbai at the age of 14, and now she's back in Mumbai with her mom and sister.

Elyse took an auto to the Church, and after reaching there she noticed that the church is very much different from what she saw 8 years ago. Then she entered the church and prayer was going on. Elyse sat on the second row bench where she used to sit since childhood. The church father came and called her out by name, and that was surprising for Elyse.

"So it took you these many years to come here, Elyse?"

"Oh Jesus, father, you still remember me and my name. This is a surreal moment for me. I got goosebumps. How are you, father?"

"I'm all good Elyse, everyday i used to remember you and your family. The reason today we are happy and enlightened is because of your family. So how can I forget you all."

"We did what we had to do, father. But nature and mother Mary weren't kind with my dad. She took him so early from us. We suffered a lot in our native after our dad left us, now we shifted here and hoping to lead a new life with happiness, so to get that i came here today!"

"Remember this Elyse, if something bad happens to us. Then something good is going to happen! So anytime you can expect that to arrive in your life."

"Hope that happens soon, father. Then say what all I missed about Mumbai in the past 8 years?"

"Nothing enough has changed here Elyse, except the people. Earlier people used to visit church and for prayers without fail. Now after the pandemic, everybody is sticking with online meets and prayers sessions."

"So you're trying to say that you've lost the actual glow and vibe of people visiting Church, isn't it father?"

"Yes, Elyse. We almost tried everything to bring back all our people. But none succeeded, and we are still figuring out what will make them come back."

"I think I have an idea, father. Shall I propose it?"

"Sure Elyse, why not. Let me hear what you got!"

"I think you're aiming for the old school people. Why aim for old gen people, why not bring our gen-Z people and arrange a fest! This will bring in more people which is attention grabbing!"

"Elyse, this is not business. We are providing peace and spirituality. This is not about money dear."

"I never talked in terms of money, father. More the people arrive, the more they recommend it. It's about engagement, father. Then this might lead to more people coming face to face rather than sitting in front of the screen. Meeting people is the best thing! So this might work father. Arrange a fest with the new generation kids as organizers, then see how this church will be filled."

"Hope this works, Elyse. If everything goes well then I'll be the happiest person ever to be!"

"Everything will be fine, father. Jesus is with us!"

"Yes, what about your marriage Elyse?"

"Thanks, father. I would rather not talk about it. I'll leave now!"

"I'm sorry if I've asked something wrong, Elyse."

"It's fine, i'll be fine Father,"

"Every problem in this universe is solvable, Elyse. You can confess here if you have to. Jesus will help you out!"

"I don't think Jesus will help me out to solve the phase I'm going through, father."

"Hope you find the person who can solve your problem very soon, Elyse."

"Thanks for the wishes, father!"

Elyse left the church and started walking towards the bandstand sea face view. The past memories made her feel uncomfortable there in the church, and thought she might get some peace of mind and silence in the seashore so Elyse walked to reach there as fast as possible.

# CHAPTER THREE

# YEAH, IT'S BEEN A LONG TIME!

Shantanu reached the bandstand and sat near the rocks, he could feel comfortable and light by hearing the sound of the sea waves. He couldn't accept what happened with him and he was looking at the chats of his with Poorna. Someone came and sat nearby to Shantanu, it was Elyse.

Elyse felt relieved after watching the sea face view in a silent environment where only she could hear the sound of the marching sea waves crashing on the rocks. The question which was raised by the church father made her recollect all the past memories, the bad ones more!

Almost both of them sat there for half an hour and they didn't give a glance on eachother. Then they both stood up and were about to leave that place. Elyse was the first to leave and Shantanu waited till the woman leaves, by going a few steps ahead Elyse landed on the slippery surface which made her fall down.

Luckily Shantanu held her from the back and helped her to come out of the slippery surface and that was the moment when both of them looked at each other's face, eyes and eyes met each other after a long time, and both recognized that both of them were familiar with each other at some point of time.

"Some of these places like this might be slippery mam, use the torch on your phone to walk out from here safely."

"Thanks for helping, and please don't call me mam. Feels like I'm aged! You can call me Elyse."

"Fine Elyse, Keep moving on the drier parts of the rocks."

"Yeah, you won't say your name in return?"

"The name is Shantanu, you can call me Shan!"

"I know someone with that name, someone special!"

"I'm sure that I'm not the person whom you think of, Elyse."

"Probably it may be, Shan"

Both of them exchanged a few words with each other and walked out to the exit.

"Mr. Shan, can you help me out?"

"What can I do for you? Elyse?"

"I'm new to this city and I'm not that familiar with bus numbers and stops available to reach my destination. Can you help out with this, Shan?"

"Sure, I'll walk you through to the bus stop you need to depart, Elyse."

At that moment both Elyse and Shantanu got a sense of feeling that they both knew each other but were a bit hesitant to ask about each other. They reached the bus stop and Shantanu broke the ice between them.

"I don't know whether to ask this, are you new to the city, Elyse?"

"Actually I'm revisiting Mumbai after 8 years. I came here for work purposes. So I was already a Mumbaikar, Shan!"

"Wait, have you done your schooling from LAS?"

"Yes, and are you the Shantanu who was the famous athlete of the school?"

"Buddy, you're Elyse Charles!"

"And you're Shantanu Rajsekhar!"

"Oh my god, Elyse. It's been a long time, and now you decided to show up?"

"Nothing like that Shan, family problems made us leave this city and our friends. And yeah, it's been a long time and you have changed a lot!"

"Glad we met now Elyse, first of all how are you? How's family?"

"We are doing good now, my father passed away last year. So we decided to move back here and lead a peaceful life."

"I'm sorry about your father, Elyse."

"Thanks, Shan! What about you? How are you doing and how's your family?"

"As usual, my family is doing well enough, and I just landed a job today!"

"That's great news, Shan! You have to celebrate this!"

"I don't think I'm in a mood to celebrate this, Elyse."

"You don't worry about anything, today's treat is mine, Shan! And you just have to come with me now!"

"Elyse, no need for it now, you'll be late to home. It's already 10 now."

"I'll inform my mom, you just be quiet and come with me!"

Elyse was very much into celebrating Shantanu's success, so she and Shan took an auto and went to the nearby cafe!

# CHAPTER FOUR

# THE TWIST OF FATE!

Shantanu was thinking where Elyse was taking him for the treat and celebration. Unfortunately she took him to the same cafe where he never wanted to visit after what happened with him a few hours ago.

"Elyse, this place might be costly. I think we should go somewhere cheaper."

"Are you saying that I can't afford this place and treat, Shan?"

"No no, sorry! I didn't mean that way, Elyse."

"Then you come with me, as i said today is on me! I'll handle it, Shan!"

"Fine, go ahead. But still reconsider Elyse."

"You shut up and come with me now, Shan!"

The waiter noticed that Shantanu had arrived with his girlfriend at the cafe, so he arranged everything as planned. Elyse and Shantanu chose the center table in the cafe, and were waiting for the waiter to come and take order.

But Shantanu was very much nervous because he had planned a surprise for Poorna, but the waiter may mistake Elyse as his girlfriend and surprise her. And that will be an awkward moment for him.

"Elyse, now also there's a chance to change some other cafe or hotel for your treat."

"Why are you so nervous now, Shan? Is someone you know present here and that is making you uncomfortable?"

"No, there's nothing like that. I've heard from my friends that this place is very costly compared to other cafes in town."

"Shan, I think I'm making you uncomfortable with my presence. If you feel so, say it. I'll leave from here."

"Elyse, please don't say that. I would never feel like that about you! Fine, you'll see in a few minutes and will get to know why I'm a bit disturbed here."

"Let me see then, I won't judge you for what's gonna happen, Shan!"

As expected, the waiter with a few other waiters came to the table where Elyse and Shantanu were waiting to give orders.

"Mam, can we have a minute of yours?"

"Sure, why not! I think this is arranged by Mr. Shantanu?"

"Yes, mam. This is for you, and all these are for you."

Elyse received the special cone coffee and there were writings embedded on it. It was "will you be my better half, sweetheart?" In it, after seeing this there was a smile on Elyse's face but there was horror mode on Shantanu's face. Elyse saw Shantanu and smiled back again and thanked the waiters for the surprise.

"Thank you so much for this surprise, it really means a lot."

"Mam, you haven't given your word to Mr. Shantanu sir?"

"I'll say to him personally, not openly here! But thanks for whatever you did for me and presented here for me!"

"It's our pleasure mam, enjoy the coffee!"

It was a very awkward moment for Shantanu, because this was planned for someone else and it got displayed to someone. Elyse was impressed with Shantanu's plan and creativity and started to ask about it.

"So it clearly seems that I've interfered with something of your special moment, Shantanu. Isn't it?"

"It was supposed to happen an hour ago, it just got delayed and happened with the wrong person. This is very embarrassing right now. You still wanna sit here, Elyse?"

"I agree that something went wrong and only you and I know about this, not the people here know that. So there's nothing to be embarrassed about. Chill Shantanu!"

"You don't know what I went through a few hours ago. It's still piercing my heart, and I'm just acting fake in front of you! You won't understand this Elyse."

"Every problem is solvable if you open up the problem with someone you believe in. Not to me but the person you trust more than anything! So we can leave this place, and go to our homes, Shantanu."

"I don't wanna ruin the celebration of yours because of me, Elyse. You order something which you like and I'll have the same with you."

"Okay, I'll go with a red velvet cake with cone coffee!"

# CHAPTER FIVE

# SHAN, POORNA, LOVE, END!

Elyse understood that something went wrong with Shantanu, and she thinks that because of her it might have gone wrong. So Elyse starts to ask about the plan and to whom it was planned.

"Is she gonna come now, Shan?"

"She was supposed to but I think it's not anymore, Elyse."

"May I know what happened? If you feel okay and comfortable to share with me, Shan."

"You know life is supposed to be filled with surprises, Elyse. But I think God has turned a hard back while writing mine."

"I know you have gone through something terrible, if you open up more I may help you in that, Shan!"

"Her name was Poorna, I met her in my college days. We first started our conversation at an event, from there we started to hangout frequently, texted each other a lot and in our final year we got to know that we love each other."

"I'm happy for you, Shan. But what happened now? This surprise was supposed to be for Poorna, right?"

"Yes, Elyse. It was for her, but fate wasn't with me. After the pandemic she wasn't the Poorna I knew, her attitude, behavior and characteristics changed a lot and I also got to know from a mutual friend of ours that her parents are seeing an alliance for her."

"But you still loved her, Shan? Even though you got to know about the alliance matter?"

"Because I used to believe in her, I thought she would not leave me for any reason. But today she called me up and said that our relationship is done, it's the end."

"But why? You are the person every girl in our school wants to be their boyfriend, you're a worthy opponent to the other boys in our school, Shan."

"You can say these things to comfort me, Elyse. But she had other thoughts and plans. Poorna thought I'm not financially strong enough to take care of her. And I was a jobless person and couldn't afford her gifts like her friends' boyfriends."

"I think she didn't love you for your character Shan, she might have just used you because you were handsome and it might give her some popularity among her friends."

"Please don't say that, Elyse. I know how my Poorna is, sorry.. She was.. Let's not talk about it anymore."

"I'm sorry Shan, I didn't know you're going through this and I simply acted like a child and dragged you here where you didn't want to be."

"It's fine, Elyse. What you'll do for my sad story, you brought me here to celebrate my success and to see a person like you who's celebrating their friend's success is very rare."

"We have been friends for 10+ years, so your success is like mine. I hope you're okay now, everybody goes through this phase, Shan. There are even more chaotic problems in the world. I'm not saying yours is not that serious, it is and it's hurting emotionally."

"I can get it Elyse, what can we do if the person we love doesn't love us back. It's better to leave them rather than bothering them."

"Yeah, you're correct. It's better to move on rather than thinking about it again and again and ruining our mental state. Everything will be fine, Shan."

"So was this your first day at work, Elyse?"

"Yes, it was Shan. It was a pretty good start today, hope it picks up the pace."

"So you didn't say why you actually left Mumbai and returned to Mumbai? If you're okay to open up about this with me, you can Elyse."

# CHAPTER SIX

# ELYSE, CHARLES, MARRIAGE, DEMISE!

Shantanu made a mistake by asking about Elyse's past. And Elyse was determined not to talk about it again anymore, but Shan is her friend and he doesn't know what happened with her. So for the first time Elyse opens up about her past happenings with Shantanu.

"Shan, i made a promise to myself that i wont talk about this topic anymore, but with you i'll share it. It's because I trust you and I want this to be between us only."

"You have my word, Elyse."

"Shan, we all have dreamt about a life which we wished for but reality has something different planned for us. It may be benefitting to some and bring sorrow to some, and with me I got only sorrow as my return gift."

"You lost your father, I can understand what you're going through, Elyse."

"My father would've been alive now if i didn't say yes to that damn decision of my family. You never say yes to your parents plan, Shan."

"I didn't get you, Elyse?"

"We left Mumbai after i completed my 10<sup>th</sup> grade, all of us in our family were confused why dad took this decision. Then after 3-4 years he opened up about leaving Mumbai. It was because I liked someone at that time and he didn't want to move ahead and create chaos in future."

"I'm sorry to say this Elyse, but that was a very dumb decision taken by your father."

"Yeah I know, but he's the father so we had to follow him. Then comes the next big decision to be taken into consideration, typical Indian marriage! My father saw a person from his workplace and talked about him getting married to me since my father knew his father for years, they were colleagues basically."

"So you accepted that decision of your father's? Did you personally feel that it was the right decision, Elyse?"

"Personally it was a no from me, but if i see my family then i had to accept. We can't make our own decisions when our family is struggling to live peacefully, Shan."

"So you're saying sacrifice is meant to be made, regardless of the future. I think you accepted it for the family, isn't it Elyse?"

"Yes, Shan. I had to, then as usual they asked dowry from my father and he also accepted what all they said to give. I think approximately around 10 Lakhs and some amount of jewelry. Mom and dad somehow managed to bring that much money and everything went well."

"Your father had a great responsibility to make your life happy and safe. What happened after that, Elyse?"

"Everybody got stuck, all because of the lockdown and my father's one and only mistake was giving the dowry amount and jewels to their family as safety, but that backfired as a nightmare. They saw another girl for him and used our money and they finished everything without telling us anything."

"My god, didn't you guys file a case on them, you have to sue them. It's all your father's hard work, and what did you do, Elyse?"

"My father was devastated after knowing this news, he just came back home from office as usual and told us this news. All of us cried a lot because we were cheated and lost all our savings. He consoled us a lot and made us feel secure by supporting us like nothing happened."

"I don't like where this is going, Elyse. Please don't say what happened next, I can't take that."

"I can't change that now, Shan. I have to say what actually happened. That night he waited till we all slept, then he went to bed. The next morning we all got up and fixed our mind that nothing happened and all was a bad dream and started our routine. But my father didn't wake up. I just heard my mom screaming my dad's name and crying heavily, he was not with us anymore. I fainted there itself and I woke up in a hospital, I then rushed home and just sat next to him. I lost the one person who was always thinking about my life, now there's no one."

"I think I have seen and heard a lot for today, mine is nothing compared to your loss, Elyse. Why do we only suffer when there's so much population in this world?"

"We just spoke it out to each other, shantanu. There are people who are keeping those within themselves and helping others with their experience."

When both confessed their past happenings, the waiter came with 2 plates of red velvet pastries. Elyse and Shantanu started to have their dessert and gave some break for their conversation.

# CHAPTER SEVEN

# I HAD A CRUSH ON YOU

Elyse really loved the cake, it was too delicious and was waiting for the special cone coffee to arrive. Meantime Elyse thought to ask about Shantanu's life before meeting Poorna and what all things he did when Elyse wasn't here in Mumbai.

"So Shan, was Poorna the only girl with whom you had a relationship or were there any other girls in your life?"

"Poorna was the only girl, there wasn't any other girl like her. But now she also changed, so I'm losing interest in getting into a relationship again."

"Come on dude, it's just your first break up. There are many more things left to see in your life. Maybe you'll get a better girl in your life, Shan."

"Whatever, so what about you Elyse? You had any relationship and what about the boy you liked in our school days?"

"I never had any relationships, but I badly wanted to be with a guy in our school. A guy with a beautiful smile and charming expressions. You'll never get to see a baby face like his, Shan."

"Wow, I've never heard or seen a girl talking about a boy whom she liked the most. But I'm still trying to think who that lucky guy is."

"It is you, Shan. It was always you, I had a crush on you!"

Shantanu was stunned after hearing that one line of Elyse. He never expected this side of story from Elyse and he never thought about her having feelings for him during school days.

"Elyse, why are you saying this now to me?"

"Because I felt so, Shan. If my dad didn't take me away from you, our friends, & Mumbai then maybe this situation might not have shown up."

"I'm so confused right now, you're saying all this after these many years, Elyse."

"Let me explain the whole thing, Shan. You might get a clear picture of it then."

"Okay, I'll listen to it, Elyse."

"We all studied together till 7th Standard, we all were the bestest group in our school. I never felt something when you were with me, but the moment I got to know that you're in another class that was the moment I started to develop feelings for you. I used to come early every morning and wait near the corridors to see you come and greet me good morning, then peeping through the window and seeing you having talks with our teachers. Then playing like a ferocious lion in our sports day and bagging most of the medals, that was the best moment to see your victory."

"You know very much better than me, I never get to know about this from anyone or i haven't seen you admiring me whenever i talk to you, how Elyse?"

"I never said this to anyone, Shan. I kept this within myself and kept admiring you a lot. The way you interact with us, the way you care for us, the way you give us respect. These all made me fall for you! When I came to confess about this but you weren't there. And my dad also got to know that I was acting differently from being normal and after that all changed forever!"

"I don't know what to say, Elyse. I'm grateful that i've been a good person with you, but i never thought of me being a reason for creating this feeling in you."

"That's nothing wrong, Shan! You were good to me at that time. So I liked you very much."

"Do you now, Elyse?"

"I always do, Shan!"

Shantanu was confused at that moment. The coffee for both were served. Elyse was feeling relieved after expressing her feelings for Shantanu after 10 long years. But Shantanu was still hesitant and not able to talk forward normally with her.

"So you got anything to say, Shan?"

"I think it's time to leave, you're already late now. I'll catch a cab for you."

"That's all you got to say? You don't have anything else to share, Shan?"

"Uh.. thanks for the treat and thanks for meeting after these many years. We'll be in touch, this is my number. You can call me anytime for any help needed."

"Thank you, Shan. I appreciate your concern."

Elyse expected some answer from Shantanu, but he wasn't in a state to talk with her face to face. He booked a cab for her, waited till the cab arrived. Elyse called her mom and informed about she's about to leave the place and will come in a cab. The ride came, Shantanu opened the door for her, Elyse got in, the door closed, Shan's and Elyse's eyes met with a different feel for the first time.

# CHAPTER EIGHT

# WILL YOU BE MY BETTER HALF?

Elyse reached home, got freshed up and went directly to her bedroom and was just staring on her phone and waiting for Shantanu's message. The same was with Shantanu, he was just waiting for the message from Elyse.

After waiting for a couple of minutes, Shantanu couldn't resist and he messaged Elyse. And Elyse got a notification sound, she grabbed her phone quickly from the table and both started chatting.

"You reached home, Elyse?"

"Yeah, what about you, Shan?"

"Me too, so you haven't slept yet, Elyse?"

"Yeah, i'll have a glass of milk now and will go to sleep."

"Nice, okay so... Yeah sleep well, Elyse."

"I know you came up with something to ask, so it's better you ask it now itself Shan, don't hide it."

"Okay, what are you expecting me to say, Elyse?"

"About what?"

"You confessed your feelings right? And you expected some answer for that from me, so I'm asking what answer you're expecting, Elyse."

"How would I know what answer you're going to give? I was just curious to see your reaction to my feelings I had for you, Shan. And I never asked you a question, did you?"

"Okay, I made a mistake by not saying anything to that but didn't you partially propose to me there, Elyse?"

"What do you think, did I Shan?"

"That's the thing i can't figure out, that's why i texted you to get to know, Elyse."

"You go to sleep Shan, you'll get a clear picture afterwards."

"Can we meet tomorrow? Same cafe at 6 PM, Elyse?"

"Why so? Is there anything important to talk about, Shan?"

"Yes, you'll get my answer tomorrow! I'm sure about this Elyse. Treat is mine tomorrow!"

"Fine, good night Shan. I'll be there at 6 PM."

"Thanks, good night Elyse."

Elyse was curious about what Shantanu would say tomorrow, and Shantanu was thinking about whether his decision would be correct or not.

The next day, Elyse finished all her work and left the office earlier than usual and took an auto for the cafe. Sharply at 6 PM she reached the cafe and was expecting Shantanu to be in there waiting for her but he wasn't.

Elyse thought he would've been stuck in traffic so she waited in the lawn area for him to arrive. It was one hour Elyse was standing there and Shantanu hadn't come yet. The waiter noticed Elyse and requested her to come in and sit until her companion came.

Finally Shantanu came in a rush after so much delay and entered the cafe, Elyse was a bit mood off because he was late, and stared at him with anger.

"I'm sorry Elyse, I'm quite late. Did you order something for you?"

"You said our meeting is at 6 PM, and I came before time and waited for you! But you're coming like nothing happened! What are you up to Shan?"

"Well, I needed some time to think about today's event and what I should say to you now. So I spent all night thinking about it and I slept for a long time and here I'm late because of that. Yes, I'm late Elyse, and I'm sorry for making you wait so long."

"Wait, this isn't you. This is not the Shan I saw yesterday and now you're totally different and your face looks fresh than yesterday night! How has this tremendous change?"

"Elyse?"

"Yes.. Shan?"

"Will you be my better half, Elyse?"

Elyse was totally stunned after what Shantanu said, she never expected this sentence to be said by the person she admire the most, she's very much happy and excited to say yes to him from the bottom of her heart but mind is saying to stop this and talk with further about why he said that line.

"Well, that was so fast, Shan. But why me? And how do you think I'll accept it?"

"When I met Poorna, I wasn't me. I changed myself to keep her happy and support her in all terms. But I felt I'm missing myself and could be in my normal form. But still I continued to be like that, thinking to myself that something has to be changed for your partner. And yesterday she broke up everything what i had built for her."

"So what did you get to know from that, Shan?"

"I had love for her and she had priorities in that, a greedy approach. "

"Then, what's now, Shan?"

"She just saw my wealth, and she was with me for maybe for a couple of years. But you were with me for almost a decade, and you are the only person who knows about me very well and most importantly you liked my innocence and the way I am. So why should I worry about the person who left me like anything and I live happily my further life with the person who was almost on the verge of proposing a long time ago. What do you say, Elyse?"

"So what if I broke up with you? You'll do the same thing right again searching for the next better person than me. Isn't it Shan?"

"You will not leave me, Elyse. I'm sure about it."

"How do you know Shan? You got any proof for this?"

"You spent the last evening with me, not even thinking about anything. That shows how much you trusted me and I'll be loyal and respectful to your trust."

"This seems very awkward isn't it Shan? Yesterday you were heartbroken but today you're proposing to me? How can I believe you?"

"I was heartbroken because I loved the wrong person, and on the same day I met the person who loved me more than I expected someone to be. And I got a sense of belief in that person, I trust you Elyse, and I like you and I wish to live my further life with you.."

"What if I say No? What if I reject you, Shan?"

"You won't, dear, your eyes have already accepted me. Your face is just acting like it's normal, but your eyes are filled with joy and happiness waiting to enjoy the moment!"

Elyse realized that this is her moment, her all time wish came true and she's going to be the person she admired and wanted to love more and more she could.

"Then, propose to me now, Shan!"

"I think I just did a few minutes ago, you didn't get it Elyse?"

"You did a typical proposal, but I want to see your style of proposal. The surprise one.."

Both Elyse and Shantanu smiled at each other. He called the waiter to bring the surprise, the waiter also bought the same Red velvet cake on a plate in which it was written "Will you be my better half, Elyse?"

"Yes, I do accept my love, Shan! But when did this arrangement happen?"

"Actually I was late because of this planning, so shall we go somewhere to enjoy our day Elyse?"

"As you wish Shan!"

Finally, Shantanu met the love of life, Elyse. Both enjoyed having the pastries and *a love happened over coffee!*

# Thank You!

It's been an year i haven't released a book in that period. But you readers stayed with me, supported me at every point of time i feel low or sad. I made up mind again, focused on a new path now and i'll try my best to give you more and more interesting stories with lovable characters. Thank You All !